"BORING things are **IMPORTANT**, too," says Mum.

Bluey thinks that if boring things were important, then they'd be more **FUN**.

Dad bursts in.

"Let's go for a swim in Uncle Stripe's pool!" yells Dad.

"Yeah!" cry the girls.

"Don't forget the swim stuff," calls Mum. But Bluey, Bingo, and Dad are already rushing out the door and into the car.

"Mum is such a fusspot. She always makes us do **BORING** things," says Bluey.

"She does," says Dad.

When they get to Uncle Stripe's, Bluey leaps down onto the footpath. It's hot!

Bluey and Bingo don't have their sandals.

OW OW!

EE EE!

So Dad ends up carrying them.

I'm a GIRAFFE!

Then it's time for Bluey and Bingo to put on their rashies and sunscreen. But Dad's forgotten them.

"We'll just have to stay in the shady bit, and we'll put our hats on," says Dad.

"What hats?" asks Bluey.

Bluey does a cannonball into the pool.
This is going to be **FUN!**

Bingo wants to jump in, too.
"Dad, can I have my floaties?" she asks.

"Sorry, Squirt, I didn't bring them," says Dad.

Bingo's not sure about the crawly thing, either!

Bluey wants to swim all the way to the other end of the pool. But she can't go into the sunny bit.

"You've got no sunscreen on," reminds Dad.

"Dad, is the shady bit going to get **BIGGER** or SMALLER?" asks Bluey.

"Ah . . . **BIGGER**, for sure," says Dad.

"I meant SMALLER," says Dad.

The pool doesn't seem
that much **FUN** anymore.

DAD, I'M BORED.

DAD, I'M COLD.

DAD, I'M FREEZING.

DAD, I'M HUNGRY.

DAD, I'M STARVING.

15

"Okay. Can everyone stop saying 'Dad'!" says Dad.

"I think Dad is actually **BORING**. Mum is way more **FUN!**" declares Bluey.

A warm voice floats into the pool area.

"Oh, that's nice to hear," says Mum. "I brought all the swim stuff you left behind."

MUM! MUM!

Mum even remembered to bring morning tea.

After they've eaten,
Mum helps Bluey put
on some sunscreen.

And Dad helps Bingo
with her floaties.

19

"So **BORING** things are **IMPORTANT** sometimes, then?" asks Mum.

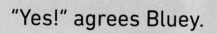

"Yes!" agrees Bluey.

Goggles mean
Bluey can play
torpedo.

Floaties mean Bingo can
escape from the crawly thing.

And sinkies take you to the very bottom of the pool . . .

. . . where you can see all sorts of things.

It's a hot summer's day, and Bluey wants to know what the family is going to do.

"Nothing, until you've cleaned your teeth," says Mum. But Bluey doesn't want to.

THAT'S BORING!

BLUEY
THE POOL

PENGUIN YOUNG READERS LICENSES
An imprint of Penguin Random House LLC, New York

First published in Australia by Puffin Books, 2021

First published in the United States of America by Penguin Young Readers Licenses,
an imprint of Penguin Random House LLC, New York, 2022

This book is based on the TV series *Bluey*.

Visit us online at penguinrandomhouse.com.

Printed in the United States of America

ISBN 9780593385685

16 15 14 13   COMM